CAST OF CHARACTERS

STEPHIE—pregnant, trying to make the right decisions for herself and those she cares about

JASON—Stephie's boyfriend, torn between his responsibility to Stephie and the baby and the promise of a college basketball career

DONTAY—in foster care while his parents are in prison, feeling unwanted both inside and outside the system

CARMEN—arrested on a DUI charge, waiting in a juvenile detention center for a judge to hear her case

HARRIS—disowned by his father after disclosing that he's gay, living in his car and taking care of himself

KATIE—angry at her mother's loyalty to an abusive stepfather, losing herself in long hours of work and school

KEESHA—struggling to find a way to take care of herself and protect her younger brother after her father kicks her out

HELEN FROST

KEESHA'S HOUSE

SQUARE
FISH

FARRAR STRAUS GIROUX

NEW YORK

SQUARE
FISH

An imprint of Macmillan Publishing Group, LLC

Library of Congress Cataloging-in-Publication Data
Frost, Helen, 1949–
Keesha's house / Helen Frost.
p.   cm.
Summary: Seven teens facing such problems as pregnancy, homosexuality, and abuse each
describe in poetic forms what caused them to leave home and where they found home again.
ISBN 978-0-312-64127-6
[1. Teenagers—Fiction.   2. Home—Fiction.   3. Family problems—Fiction.   4. Interpersonal
relations—Fiction.   5. Poetry.]   I. Title.
PZ7.F9205 Ke 2003
[Fic]—dc21
2002022698

Originally published in the United States by Farrar Straus Giroux
First Square Fish Edition: January 2013
Square Fish logo designed by Filomena Tuosto
Book designed by Barbara Grzeslo
fiercereads.com

11 13 15 17 19 20 18 16 14 12

AR: 4.4 / LEXILE: NP

Dedicated with love
to my sister
Barbara

contents

PART I

HOW I SEE IT

NOW THiS BaBY   STEPHIE

My parents still think I'm their little girl.
I don't want them to see me getting bigger,
bigger every week, almost too big to hide it now.
But if I don't go home, where can I go?
Jason said, *You could get rid of it.* I thought of how he tossed
the broken condom in the trash, saying, *Nothing*

will happen. Now this baby is that nothing,
growing fingers in the dark, growing toes, a girl
or boy, heart pulsing. Not something to be tossed
aside, not nothing. Love and terror both grow bigger
every day inside me. Jason showed me where to go
to take care of it. I looked at him and said, *I can't.* Now

he isn't talking to me, and if he won't talk now,
I know what to expect in six months' time—nothing.
His family doesn't know about the baby. When I used to go
there every day, his mom would say, *It's nice to have a girl
around the house.* But they have bigger
dreams than this for Jason. All my questions are like wind-tossed

papers in the street, and after they've been tossed
around, rain comes, and they're a soggy mess. Now
I'm hungry. I had a doughnut, but I need a bigger
meal. I'm not prepared for this. I know nothing
about living on my own. At school there's this girl
I know named Keesha who told me there's a place kids go

and stay awhile, where people don't ask questions. I go,
Yeah, sure, okay. I kind of tossed
my head, like I was just some girl
who wouldn't care. But now
I wish I'd asked her the exact address. (Nothing
wrong with asking.) To lots of girls, it's no big

deal to have a baby. They treat it like a big
attention getter—when the baby's born, they go
around showing it off to all their friends. But nothing
like this ever happens in my family. Mom and Dad won't toss
me out, or even yell at me, if I go home right now.
But how can I keep acting like the girl

they think I am—a carefree teenage girl with nothing
big to worry me. As for what I've started thinking now—
don't go there. Heads is bad; tails is worse: like that no-win coin toss.

what's right? JASON

Coach keeps asking me what's wrong.
I missed the free throw, cost our team the game.
I thought I could count on you, he said,
quiet, really puzzled, those dark eyes steady,
looking through me. How can I say, Forget
the championship, forget the scholarship, college

is out of the question? And without college—
what? You want to know what's wrong?
I want to know what's right. I can't forget
Stephie's eyes, the light through her tears. The old game
plan won't work now. *Are you two going steady?*
Coach asked. He was serious. He said,

She's a lovely girl, Jason. All I can say
is, times have changed. In his day, you went to college,
married the lovely girl you'd gone steady
with for four years. Nothing went wrong
like this. I wish I could play the game
like that. I wish I could forget

about this baby. But I can't forget
the night it happened. Stephie said
she loved watching me play in the big game;
she loved the brains that got me into college,
but there was more than that. I was wrong
if I thought that was all she saw in me. Steady

light in her eyes. I want to be steady
for her now. But I'm not. I can't. Forget
it. It's all turning out wrong.
When I drove her past the clinic, she said,
You want me to kill our baby so you can go to college,
play basketball, be a big hero in every big game?

Those words: *Kill our baby.* No. This is not a game.
I need some kind of job, a steady
income. I could stay here and go to college
part-time, but I'd have to forget
about my basketball career. Whoever said
these are the best years of your life was wrong.

But Stephie's also wrong. I don't think everything's a game.
I just can't seem to say, *Yes, I'll be the kind of steady*
father I should be. It's hard to forget about college.

i found a pLace   KEESHA

Stephie walked by this afternoon, holding
her umbrella in front of her face.
When it rains like this, all day, into the night,
that's when you need a home
more than you need your pride. She still
goes home to her folks, but she's scared

of something. I can tell when someone's scared
and I can usually guess what it's about. She's been holding
her books in front of herself, and she still
wears that heavy jacket, even when the weather's good. Her face
clouds over whenever it's time to go home.
She'll go home again tonight, but one night

soon, she'll find her way here. Just watch—Sunday night
or a week from Tuesday, she'll show up scared,
like she's the first girl that ever ran from home.
I know how it is. The night I ran off, holding
on to my picture of Mama, like her face
could talk to me or something, I still

believed someone would come after me. I still
thought the cops or *somebody* would look for me all night,
and Dad would say he didn't mean it. His face
when I left, so tight and dark. I'm scared
when his eyes flash like that—*Don't come back.* Holding
his bottle like a gun. What would a real home

be like? An everybody-sit-down-at-the-table home?
I remember when Mama was still
alive, sitting on that brown couch holding
Tobias. He had an earache, he cried all night,
and she stayed up and tried to quiet him. She was scared
of Dad. I remember his face,

so angry when one of us cried. And her face,
softer when he wasn't home.
I'm never going to live like that, scared
of what a man will do to me. I'm still
in school. I found a place to sleep at night,
and I'm smart. You won't see me holding

a baby anytime soon. I'm still trying to hold
my own life together. I face each night
by calling this place home. No one's going to see me acting scared.

HOW i see it   DONTAY

They'll be sayin' I ran
off, but that ain't how I see it. To me—
I went to Carmen's house
where all my friends chill out,
and when I called home for a ride,
my foster dad said, *You got there on your own, son;*

you should be able to get home. They call me *son*
like that. But if I was, they'd run
out in that fancy car and give me a ride
when I need one. It ain't no home to me.
It look like one, sittin' on that green lawn, out
in the suburbs. My caseworker say, *This house*

has everything. Four bedrooms, three baths, the house
of your dreams. Sound like she sellin' it. Their real son
has a bathroom to hisself, and a sign that says KEEP OUT
on his door. He got the whole crib on lock, runnin'
the whole show. But me—
I feel like I'm beggin' if I ask for a ride.

I hafta ask if I can eat! I got a ride
home last Thursday, and when I went in, the house
was quiet. They was all done eatin', nothin' left for me.
My foster mom said, *Sorry, son,*
you need to learn, if you want to run
around with those kids, and stay out

past suppertime, you can't expect us to go out
of our way to feed you. Where they live, you need a ride
to go get food. You can't just run
to the corner for a sandwich or go to a friend's house
and eat with them. Carmen's grandmama call me *son*
too, sometimes, but if I'm hungry at their house, she'll feed me.

So now I don't know what to do. It's gonna look like me
messin' up again. But to me—they locked me out!
If I had my own key like their son,
I coulda got in last night when I finally got a ride
from Carmen. It was midnight, and the house
was dark. Carmen thought I'd gone inside. I tried to run

and catch her, but she didn't see me standin' out
there in the dark street—no house, no food, no ride.
I didn't run off. I shivered in the backyard, waitin' for the sun.

some Little thing CARMEN

I'll be sixteen in seven months,
and I know how to drive.
When Dontay had to find his own ride home,
Grandmama was asleep. I know where she keeps
her keys. I borrowed them and drove as careful as I could
out to that house he's stayin' at. By the time I left

him off, it was after curfew. I turned left
on Main Street, thinkin' 'bout the time we all got stopped last month
in that same place, thinkin' I could
go a different way. Shoulda done that, but I thought I'd drive
that short way, take my chances. Tried to keep
an eye out, but I got stopped before I made it home.

That is, to Grandmama's house—what I call home
since Mama and her boyfriend left
for Cincinnati. I keep
thinkin' she'll be back, but it's five months
now, and I've about stopped hopin' she'll drive
up any minute. I guess it could

happen—prob'ly won't, but could.
Anyhow, for now, Grandmama's house is home.
Or was until she woke up to flashin' lights and saw the cops drive
up. They gave her back her keys, told her I was DUI. Left
me handcuffed in their car tryin' not to cry. I'll prob'ly get two months
this time. Don't know why I keep

on gettin' in this kind of trouble. I keep
tryin' to do right—thought I could
help out with this month's
rent. Now it looks like I won't be home
or makin' any kind of money for a while. I'll miss what's left
of school, or at least too much to make up. This could drive

you crazy: Just try to do some little thing like drive
a friend that needs a ride, and you keep
findin' yourself locked up, nothin' left
to do but sit around thinkin' how you could
be out with friends—or home.
You think about that stuff for months,

and when those months are finally over, everything you left
behind is different. You feel like jumpin' in the nearest car and drivin'
outta town, keepin' goin' till you find someplace that feels like home.

that one word   HARRIS

I got invited to the winter dance.
Think how that's supposed to be: Mom, Dad,
there's someone I'd like you to meet,
someone special in my life, someone
who loves me as much as I love him.
Freeze frame on that one word: Did you say

him? I used to try to think of how I'd say
it, how I'd let them know there'd be no dancing
at my wedding, no grandkids. Finally I just told them about him
and watched my world explode. What it meant to Dad
was that he didn't know me. I turned into someone
he's hated all his life. He wouldn't meet

my friend. *Why would I want to meet
the person who ruined your life?* I couldn't say,
No, Dad, I ruined his. They couldn't imagine just someone
I loved who loved me. Now Mom and Dad and I can't dance
around the subject like we used to. Dad
said if I didn't have enough respect for him

to *act normal*, how could I expect him
to keep supporting me? I couldn't meet
his eyes when he said that. I was ashamed of Dad
and myself at the same time. I didn't say
much, but after that, the winter dance
seemed like a childish game. Overnight, I became someone

different—older, tougher, on my own. Someone—
me—with no parents to support him.
I was scared enough to ask a girl to the dance,
thinking I could bring her home to meet
my parents. Maybe they'd let me come back. I'd say,
It was just something I went through—really, Dad,

it isn't true. But she said no. Anyway, Dad
would never have believed me. I can't pretend to be someone
I'm not. No matter what Mom might say
(and she's not saying much), to him
I might as well be dead. There's just no way to meet
halfway on this. I didn't go to the dance.

What made me think I could have danced with him
in public? Now I can't even say his name out loud. Dad
scared me into breaking up. I don't even want to meet someone.

my choice   KATIE

I sleep in my sleeping bag in a room
with a lock in the basement of the place
on Jackson Street. And I feel safe.
If Keesha wants to talk to me, she knocks
first, and if I want to let her in, I do.
If I don't, I don't. It's my choice.

There's not too much I really have a choice
about. Mom would say I chose to leave my room
at home, but that's not something anyone would do
without a real good reason. There's no place
for me there since she got married. Like, one time, I knocked
her husband's trophy off his gun safe,

and he twisted my arm—hard. I never feel safe
when he's around. I finally asked my mom to make a choice:
him or me. She went, *Oh, Katie, he'll be fine.* Then she knocked
on our wood table. I blew up. I stormed out of the room
and started thinking hard. In the first place,
I know he won't *be fine.* I didn't tell her what he tries to do

to me when she works late. In a way, I want to, but even if I do,
she won't believe me. She thinks we're safe
in that so-called nice neighborhood. *Finally, Katie, a place
of our own.* And since she took a vow, she thinks she has no choice
but to see her marriage through. No room
for me, no vow to protect *me* if he comes knocking

on my door late at night. He knocks
and then walks in when I don't answer. Or even when I do
answer: *Stay out! This is my room
and you can't come in!* I could never be safe
there, with him in the house. So, sure, I made a choice.
I left home and found my way to this place,

where I've been these past two weeks. And I found a place
to work, thirty hours a week. Today Mom knocked
on the door here. She wanted to talk. I told her, *You made your choice;
I made mine.* She wondered what she could do
to get me to come home. But when I said, *It's not safe
for me as long as he's there,* she left the room.

My choice is to be safe.
This room is dark and musty, but it's one place
I do know I can answer *no* when someone knocks.

PART II

WHITE WALLS

i hate to be the one   STEPHIE

It's Friday night. When I left home this morning,
Mom said, *We need to talk.*
She noticed that I couldn't eat my breakfast
and she looked at me long and hard—that mix
of sad and angry that I hate.
I can't face her. I'm not going home.

They probably think I've gone home
with Jason. I saw him this morning
before school, talking to a girl we both used to hate.
I walked away before he saw me. Let him talk
to her. My feelings about him are so mixed-
up right now. He used to be so sweet, eating breakfast

with his tousled hair and sleepy eyes. Breakfast
at their house is different than at home.
They're *peaceful*. If his brother mixes
a can of juice in a saucepan and leaves it out all morning,
nobody complains. And nobody expects you to talk
to them if you don't want to. Mom would hate

it. She likes everything in order. Dad too. They both hate
it if we haven't cleared away our breakfast
by eight o'clock, even on weekends. They talk
about how kids should have a home
where they know what to expect. Every morning
Mom gets up first, makes coffee, gets out a mix

of pancakes or bran muffins. Sometimes I watch her mix
it, like it's part of her job, like *I hate*
this job, but someone has to do it. This morning
she was saying, *If I get up and make you breakfast*
I expect you to eat it. I go, *Sure, Mom.* Then she goes, *I want you home*
after school today. We need to talk.

I'm afraid of what she wants to talk
about. I don't want to mix
her words about this baby with my own. Home
to her and Dad means perfect, and I hate
to be the one to shatter that. Only—where will I eat breakfast
in the morning?

Oh, Mom . . . it isn't just the talk I hate.
It's how we have to mix it up with breakfast.
Can't we just relax at home some morning?

surpriseð to hear myseLf JASON

Stephie's gone. I went over Friday night
after the game, and her brother seemed surprised.
He said, *We thought she was at your house.*
She used to do that sometimes. If it got late,
we'd pull out the couch and make a bed
for her, and then we'd go to school

together in the morning. Friday she wasn't at school.
I didn't think much of it, but that night
I really wanted to talk. *Maybe she went to bed
early*, I said. Her brother looked surprised
again. He shook his head. I went home. Then late
that night, her dad showed up at my house,

frantic. Everyone at their house
was out searching for her. They'd called the school
principal at home and found out Stephie had been absent. And late
a lot these past few weeks. Her dad said, *Son, last night
she seemed worried. Do you know why?* I was surprised
he called me son. And I was half asleep—he got me out of bed.

He looked tired. Three a.m., he hadn't been to bed
at all, everything upside down at his house.
I told him Stephie hadn't talked to me all week. Surprised,
he wondered why. *Don't you see her every day at school?
I thought she'd been here every night!
She's been coming home late*

a lot, but we just thought she was with you! Later,
I thought about him sitting there on our couch-bed
in the middle of the night.
He looked like his whole house
had collapsed, like everything he'd learned in school
turned out false where he'd put true. I was surprised

to feel so sorry for him, even more surprised
to hear myself tell him the truth. *Her period's late,*
I said. *She's afraid the kids at school
will start to notice something.* After he'd gone, I lay in bed
thinking about them all at her house.
And where *was* Stephie in the middle of the night?

I got out of bed, drove around looking for her all night—
past the school, back and forth past her house,
surprised how much I want her back. *Is it too late?*

Questions about Joe   KEESHA

When Katie came, she kept asking questions
about Joe. Since he owns the house, she thought
he'd tell us what to do. She kept saying, *I can pay
rent. I can buy my own food. I'll work
for what I need.* There was one room upstairs with a bed
and a window, but she said she'd rather stay

in the basement room. We all stay
out of there unless she asks us in. No one asks questions
about why she keeps her door locked. The bed
in there is just a foam pad on the floor, but Katie said she thought
the room was heaven. We hardly see her, she's at work
so much. I think she's worried Joe might make her pay

some other way if she runs out of money. He says we can pay
him if we want to, but not much. Me, I want to stay
in school. I want good grades. So I just work
twelve hours a week, enough for food. I hate the questions
people ask though. Even my ex-boyfriend thought
the girls here must be going to bed

with Joe, or someone else. Not me—I won't go to bed
with anyone unless I want to. And I don't pay
for *nothin'* with *my* body! At first I thought
we should do something nice for Joe—he lets us stay
here and he doesn't ask too many questions.
So if he was tired when he got home from work

I used to cook or do some kind of work
like clean up the house. Once I made his bed
for him, like Mama used to do. That raised some questions
in his mind, I guess. He said, *Keesha, don't you pay
me no mind. Everyone deserves a place to stay.*
So now I don't give Joe much thought.

I appreciate him though. If I thought
I had to find a place to rent, I'd have to work
full-time. I know I wouldn't stay
in school. This one thing—a free bed—
makes all the difference. I can stay awake in school and pay
attention to the teachers, answer almost all their questions.

I go to school, I work, I eat okay and get to bed
on time. I thought Child Welfare might ask questions,
but as long as they don't pay attention, I can stay.

i can do it DONTAY

Ain't goin' back there. If I go get my stuff
they'll yell at me for stayin' out all night.
I'll yell back, and I know what comes next—
they call my caseworker: *This isn't working out.*
She comes and gets me, lookin' like she want
to wring my neck. We head out to CYS again. I hate that place—

all those kids waitin' to get placed
in a foster home or group home, all the stuff
they hopin' for, knowin' they ain't gettin' what they want.
Everybody act so hard all day, and then at night
you hear 'em cryin' like some cakes—not out
loud, just quiet, hopin' won't nobody notice. Everybody wonderin'
    what's next.

I been there five times, and I swore up and down, the next
time they tried to take me there, I'd find my own place.
I know I can do it. Rather live out
on my own, take my stuff
in my backpack, sleep outside at night
when summer comes. Better that than findin' out nobody wants

me. Dad and Mama gonna want
to know why I don't go to visiting hours next
week, but goin' there just makes me mad again 'bout the night
they got hemmed up. Five-O all over the place,
flashin' their badges, rumblin' through our stuff,
findin' *nothin'* and still pullin' us out,

sendin' us all different places. When I go out
to see them, Mama's so sad, and Dad just wants
to do that trial all over. He's *ragin'* about all the stuff
the lawyer didn't do. They're innocent! And here I am. What's next?
I can sleep at Jermaine and Dan's crib tonight, someplace
else this weekend. I don't mind sleepin' on the floor a night

or two. Three or four places I can spend the night
a couple times before they figure out
I got no place
to live. Stay a few days, nobody want
to know why I'm leavin', nobody surprised the next
time I show up. One good thing about all this stuff—

ain't nobody kickin' me out one night
to the next. Nobody actin' like they want
to make me change. Bad thing—no place to leave my stuff.

wHite waLLs   CARMEN

I wasn't drunk. Just one beer a couple hours
before. Never woulda got stopped
if I was an adult. Or if I was white.
That half-smoked blunt they found under the back
seat—how would I know it was there?
Coulda been there since Grandmama

bought the car, five months ago. Grandmama
wouldn't think to look for that! Visiting hours
is over, and she didn't show up. Only one there
all week was my probation officer. She stopped
by for ten minutes, said she was *so unhappy* to see me back
in here, got out a clean white

notepad and asked me for an explanation. *No little white
lies*, she said. I asked her to call Grandmama,
tell her I'm sorry, see if I can go back
there when I get outta here. That was hours
ago, and I haven't heard from either of 'em. Can't stop
thinkin' about what's gonna happen. If I can't go back there . . .

I don't know. Could be a long ways, anyhow, from here to there.
I talked to one girl today, a white
girl that's been here thirteen weeks. She stopped
thinkin' about home, she said. *Forget about your grandma.*
If she don't come to visiting hours
the first week you're here, she don't want you back.

I want my own clothes back.
My music. The food I like. I see the cars go by out there,
everybody goin' someplace. In here, hours
stretch out long, nothin' but blank white
walls to look at. I started a letter: *Dear Grandmama,*
get me out of here . . . But then I stopped

and ripped it up. I know I shoulda stopped
drinkin' that first time I got caught, back
in seventh grade. I know everything Grandmama
would say about all this. I keep thinkin' there
must be some way to make myself listen, some clear white
light I could shine into my mind those hours

when I can't see my way back
or forward, the hours I think even Grandmama
won't care if I stop livin'. These walls are *so white.*

i Look around and wonder HARRIS

Another note in my locker today: *Die,*
faggot. Scrawled in thick marker—red—
on notebook paper ripped in half,
folded to fit through those little slots.
Then later, someone twice my weight shoves me
into a table in the cafeteria. My lunch

goes flying, hits this freshman eating lunch
by herself. She looks like she's about to die,
like she thinks she's the jerk, not him. I apologize; she ignores me,
moves to another table, her face bright red.
There's so many guys like him—they have these slots
they try to fit into; anyone with half

an ounce of individuality gets crushed. Kids spend half
their time just trying to fit in. You look around the lunchroom and you can see which kids are trying for which slots—
jocks or freaks or "playas." And everyone would rather die
than be what I am. Even the thugs, wearing red
or blue, with all their drugs and guns, have more friends than me.

Do people think I'm contagious? That if they talk to me
they might turn gay? Or are they scared that half
the school would hate them too? I've read
statistics: maybe one in ten kids in that lunchroom. I look around and wonder. Kids can die
a lot of different ways if they don't fit in those slots.

Three more months of school. There's lots
of things I have to figure out. So far, Dad hasn't found me
and taken back my car. It's old, but with any luck it won't die
on me. If I can find someplace to park and sleep, that's half
the battle. I'll find a weekend job where I can get lunch,
and try for dinner shift on weekdays. I read

an ad that Pancake House is hiring. I can see myself in that red
apron, pockets filling up with tips. Come summer, whatever slots
they need I'll work—graveyard one day, lunch
the next, whatever. Only—how can they call to offer me
a job? Can I clean up and look half
decent for an interview? And not sound desperate, like I'll die

if they don't hire me? I'll go on Saturday at lunch
and see what slots they're trying to fill. I could work half
time, busing their red tables. Okay, I'm scared. But I don't plan to die.

HOUSE OF CARDS KATIE

Everything was going okay between
school, work, and living here. Just
time enough in every day, and no time
left for me to think too hard.
Then today, the city bus pulls up on schedule,
I get on, and the driver has these cards

he's giving out. I take one of the cards
and plunk down in a side seat between
a lady and a kid. The lady says, *New schedule*,
so I look at the card and I just
want to cry. Now everything that used to be easy is hard.
Getting to work takes twice the time

it used to. After school I don't have time
to change into my uniform, and we can't punch our cards
until we're ready to start working. It's hard
to change in the employee restroom in five minutes between
when the bus stops at the corner and just
exactly 3 p.m. when my shift starts. The boss won't change my schedule.

I can't change my school schedule.
So—I have three choices: get a new job and work a different time,
quit school, or get a car. Which of course I can't afford just
now. It's like one of those house-of-cards
games—if I pull one out, everything above, below, and in between
collapses. I've worked really hard

to get this all set up—it's hard
to think of doing it all again. Next summer, this schedule
will be fine, but my boss won't let up between
now and then. I asked him for ten extra minutes to give me time
to get from school to work, but he says that's not in the cards.
If I can't do just

what I'm supposed to do, just
when it should be done, too bad. *I know it's hard
for you,* he says, *but I've got a business here. Cards
of sympathy are next door at Hallmark.* My schedule
is impossible. Barely time to sleep, no time
for homework except at the bus stop between

school and work. Report cards come out in two weeks' time
and I have to work hard just to pass. My schedule
will be: school and work, work and school. No time in between.

PART III

ON THEIR OWN

i kNOw tHe vaLue JOE

I know the value of a house like this.
Old and solid, hardwood stairs and floor.
But when I showed up at Aunt Annie's door
when I was twelve—bruised, scared, clenched fists—
all I knew then was: I could stay.
As long as you need to, Joe, was what she kept
on saying, right up till she died and left
the house to me. So now that's what I say
when kids show up and I know they can't ask
for what they shouldn't have to ask for. They need
more than I can give them. I know I'm
no Aunt Annie. I ain't up to the task
of tryin' to be their legal foster dad.
But I can give them space—and space is time.

ON HER OWN   LAURA (STEPHIE'S MOTHER)

It's time to talk to Steph about the boy
who could have been her brother—maybe is
her brother. How can I describe the joy
of holding him, the morning—cold—when his
new parents—married, educated—reached
to take him from me? I don't know his name
or where (or if) he lives. My parents preached
at me. I listened. I won't do the same
to Steph. She has to do this on her own.
I know wherever Stephie is tonight
she's thinking hard about the baby, us,
herself, and Jason. She's out there alone
and I can't help. Sixteen. I know. She might
not know how much she's loved, or who to trust.

you dream about a kid Like this   COACH HARDEN

Jason hasn't told me much himself
but there's a rumor going around the team
about his girlfriend. When I heard it, I felt
sick. You coach for twenty years, you dream
about a kid like this, an athlete born
for greatness. Varsity his freshman year,
state all-star two years in a row. More
natural talent than I've ever seen here
at Marshall High. And he knows how to work
for what he wants. He could go anywhere—
free ride, recruiters calling every day.
Now what? He's not one to shirk
responsibility. He seems to care
about this girl. But you should see him play.

it would be good for him MRS. MASON
(DONTAY'S CASEWORKER)

I thought I'd finally found a good, safe place
for Dontay, far from his old friends and school,
with such a nice family, of his own race.
This summer they were going to join the pool
so he could learn to swim. *I hope he meets
new friends*, I said. It would be good for him
to know some different kids. But Dontay treats
this like a punishment. *I hate to swim*,
he says, *I hate that part of town.* He can't
seem to adapt himself. It's sad. Now
he's run off, and he'll be hard to find. Three days
since he left. I'm not sure they want
to take him back. He's good at heart. But how
can I help Dontay if he won't change his ways?

Lord, give me strength ROBERTA
(CARMEN'S GRANDMOTHER)

I got to get my own self in control
before I try to talk to Carmen. Right now
I'm so mad at everyone, the whole
world look ugly to my mind. I don't know how
LaRayne could leave her girl like that.
It ain't how she was raised—she knows what's right!
But ever since she took up with that ol' fat
ugly thing she call a man, seem like she might
do anything. Now she don't even know
her child's in trouble. Least she could do is call!
Lord knows, I want to get the child free.
I want to help her straighten out. But oh,
it's hard. Lord, give me strength to carry all
the burdens people tryin' to put on me.

can't risk taking any action MR. HYDE
(ASSISTANT PRINCIPAL)

I got a student complaint this afternoon.
A Harris Murphy claims he was harassed.
Note in his locker, incident in the lunchroom
involving Bradley Smith. We could get slapped
with a lawsuit, either way we go.
Brad's mother is a lawyer. I can't risk
taking any action until I know
the facts. This isn't drugs, where we can frisk
the suspect, search for evidence. I
gave the boy a pamphlet. My advice:
Gain some weight. Consider what you wear.
Stand up and look the bully in the eye.
I told him: *You're too young to make this choice.*
Just wait. There's lots of pretty girls out there.

Not much i can do   MRS. GOLDSTEIN
(KATIE'S ENGLISH TEACHER)

Katie used to be among the best
students in my sophomore honors class.
Her work was careful, A's on every test,
good writer, conscientious. For the last
few weeks, or maybe months—when did this start?—
her grades have fallen, first to C's, now D's.
She's not doing the reading; there's no heart
behind her writing. She's in class, but she's
half asleep, and when I ask her to stay
after school, she says sorry, she can't,
she has to be at work by three o'clock.
She didn't turn her paper in today.
It's half her midterm grade. I guess I'll grant
her extra time. She doesn't want to talk.

PART IV

THE DEEP END

across whatever secret STEPHIE

Keesha found me crying in the doughnut shop across
the street from where she lives. I was sitting there alone
late Friday night. *Stephie, is that you?*
She sat down in the booth with me. The doughnut shop
was almost empty, just one old man and me. It stays
open all night long, and it seemed safe, but I was getting kind

of nervous. Keesha's face looks hard sometimes, but she's kind-
hearted. Her eyes can look right through you. Straight across
whatever secret you might carry, she follows and stays
with you. I must have felt a little more alone
than I admitted, because when she sat down, the doughnut shop
seemed brighter. My words just simmered up. I said, *You*

won't tell anyone, will you?
She looked at me and shook her head, kind
of like nothing is a secret. She told me, *There's a shop*
that sells used baby stuff, two blocks down from here, across
from Pizza Hut. I knew about it. I'd gone in there alone
the day before, thinking, if this baby stays

with me, how will I take care of it? Keesha stayed
and talked (well, listened) for two hours. When I asked, *Where do you*
live? she brought me here. She lives here alone,
I mean no parents; the kids who live here kind
of fend for themselves, I guess. A room across
from Keesha's is empty, sort of. A guy set up a shop

to make jewelry out of colored wire, and in one corner of the shop
there's a bed. Keesha said, *No one stays*
here right now; you can use that bed. Across
the street, people were fighting, a woman was yelling, *You*
bastard! I pulled down the shade, tried not to hear. That kind
of thing, these days, makes me throw up. Keesha left me alone

and I kept thinking, Can I raise a child alone?
Do my homework every night and then go out to shop
for formula and Pampers? What kind
of mother would I be? Not one that stays
home and sings lullabies, that's for sure. Not someone you
would trust to guide a child across

the kind of world I see out there. You
can't shop for what you really need: patience, strength, a man who stays
with you. Can I even get *myself* across the years ahead? Alone?

HOme COURt   JASON

It's like I'm playing forward for one team
and guard for the other
in the final quarter of the last
game of the season. I want two things
at once—Stephie safe, back home,
trusting me like before,

and my name in the sports page headlines. Before
the game today, some of the guys on the team
helped make missing-person posters. Stephie's brother took them home
and her mom and dad and a bunch of other
people put them up. It's one of those things
where if she is okay, she'll be embarrassed, but the last

thing anyone wants is another story like the one last
year, where a girl was missing for two weeks before
anyone reported her, and then they found her body in the river. Things
like that can happen, and I'm scared. Coach said the team
could play without me if there were other
things I had to do tonight, but it's the last home

game of the season, and what could I do at home
besides wait for a call that probably won't come? In last
week's game, I messed up bad. I want another
chance to get it right before
the tournament. We've got the best team
the school's had in ten years—big things

could be ahead for us. And for me, next year. Things
I'll have to turn my back on if I stay home
with Stephie. Stay home and watch ESPN, watch the team
I could have been on, knowing I missed the last
chance I had to make it big. Sometimes before
I take a shot, all the cheering and other

sounds on the court fade out. It's like I'm in some other
place where everything
is clear and silent. When that happens, especially before
a free throw, I know I'll sink the shot. It only happens on the home
court, and the moment never lasts,
but how can I describe it? It's like the two teams

are playing *with* each other, not against, like it's home
court for everyone, and everything's okay. I used to feel (before
this baby) like Steph and I were on one team. Could that feeling last?

tHe RiveR KEESHA

So. That's that. Stephanie runs
off; her parents search until they find her,
bring her home; everyone lives happily ever after, I guess.
So much fuss about one girl. Of course I'm glad
she has a home, a brother, parents
that want her there. Whatever.

Good for Stephie. She'll be fine, whatever
happens with the baby. If she runs
into trouble, her boyfriend or her parents
will be there to help her out. This morning, when she called her
family and they came to get her, they were all so glad
to see each other. I stood back and watched. I could've guessed

it'd be exactly like this. I'm glad she's gone. Now I guess
I can get my homework done, and whatever
else I got to do today. I should be glad
(I *am* glad) I got a bed. Not every kid that runs
off is so lucky. Like that one girl that used to roll her
blankets out under the Fourth Street Bridge. I never saw no parents

look for her. No missing-person posters. Oh well. Who needs parents?
Only—sometimes, like today I guess,
I think about that girl, how no one seemed to notice her
or come and take her someplace safe. It was like, whatever
happens, happens. The river running
under that bridge still sings its glad

and endless song, whether that girl is there or not. I'm glad
I found Stephie Friday night. Before she left today, I said, *If your parents
ask about me, just say the simple truth: I'm a girl that runs
track with you. Don't tell them how I live.* I guess
I'd rather stick with what I got than take my chances on whatever
someone else might think is good for me. Some caseworker with all her

rules and regulations. I don't need her
stickin' her nose in my business. I'd be glad,
though, if I thought my father asked, just once, *Whatever
happened to Keesha?* Tried to find out where I'm at, like parents
are supposed to! Tobias knows I'm here, and I guess
if anybody asked, he'd tell them. Now I see he runs

with older kids. They're prob'ly glad he doesn't have strict parents.
Whatever they want from him, he'll do it. If Mama was alive, I guess
her heart would break. But me, I'm strong—no tears run down my face.

Low-key, keepin' quiet DONTAY

I thought I could chill at Carmen's house a couple
nights—her grandmama's usually cookin' up
some food. There's always kids and good times
over there. So I stopped by, but it was quiet—
just two of Carmen's little cousins playin'
while her grandmama was talkin' on the phone.

When she got off the phone,
she told me Carmen got locked up a couple
days ago. She said, *This time it's serious, they ain't playin'*
with her now. I asked when Carmen's court date was comin' up,
but she didn't say. She was bein' quiet,
the way old folks do sometimes

when they be really mad. Might be times
she blamin' me for Carmen's troubles. I wish I could phone
Carmen, but there ain't no way. I found a quiet
place in the downtown library, spent a couple
hours there, then came over here to see what's up
at Jermaine and Dan's. New CD's playin'

on the boom box; some girls come over; everybody playin'
'round, just chillin'. It's a good time
over here tonight; things lookin' up
for me. Jermaine got on the cordless,
called out for pizza. Dan has a couple
six-packs, and everybody feelin' pretty good. Just a quiet

group of friends together on a quiet
night. I'm tryin' to stay out of trouble, playin'
it safe, hopin' Mrs. Mason gonna get a couple
extra kids so they'll take up her time
and she'll forget about me. Every time I hear a phone
ring, I wonder if she's tracked me down, settin' up

another placement for me, or maybe makin' up
a mess of trouble, listin' all my problems in her quiet
voice, then gettin' on her cell phone,
callin' some authority or other. I'm through playin'
'round with all that drama. It's too many times
now she takes me out to meet some *nice couple*,

tries to cheer me up with all her talk about good family times.
Couple weeks or months go by, phone rings again,
I'm on my way. Nope. I'm playin' this low-key, keepin' quiet.

my inside self   CARMEN

You wanna know, for real, what keeps me alive
in here? They try to think of everything
so you can't kill yourself—Velcro shoes
instead of laces, special bags for sleepin'
so you can't make a rope out of your sheets,
and that little camera in the corner

starin' at you, seems like into every corner
of your thoughts. They think I stay alive
just 'cause they make me. I could fill a hundred sheets
of paper if I wrote down everything
they do to keep us in control, awake or sleepin'.
But it ain't that. I wake up every day, put on the shoes

they gave me, and think about the day I'll get my own shoes
back. I get way back in a corner
while my roommate's still sleepin',
and I can just see out the window. I stay alive
by lookin' hard at one tree branch. I watch everything
that happens on that branch. One day last week, sheets

of ice covered every inch of it. Sun on those ice sheets
was shinin' like glass, and I remembered those shoes
Cinderella wore. You know how in that story, everything
turns out okay when she comes out from her corner
and that glass slipper fits her? Sometimes I stay alive
by thinkin' of those stories. Rapunzel, Sleeping

Beauty. (The tangled branches in front of Sleeping
Beauty's castle—remember those? Asleep between her sheets,
almost dead, but then the girl comes back alive.)
I know they all just stories. I sure ain't got no glass shoes,
or any prince to find me in a corner,
get me out. It's just that sometimes, everything

in here makes me feel dead, and everything
alive is someplace else. Instead of sleepin'
off the hours and days, I find some corner
of my mind to keep alive. They give us two sheets
of paper, once a week, for letters, and I treat them like new shoes
to take me where I want to go. I write things down to keep my
        inside self alive.

Last night I dreamed a little squirrel was sleepin' in my shoe
in a corner of my room at Grandmama's. There was sheets
of colored light on everything. Me, Grandmama, and the squirrel
        was all alive.

i ᴅon't caLL tHis steaLing HARRIS

I need a sleeping bag and a change of clothes.
I need some food.
I know where my parents hide the house key
and where they keep $100, in case
of an emergency. I know when they're at work.
And I know my rights.

They don't have the right
to throw me out with just the clothes
I'm wearing. I might not start work
for a couple weeks, and I need food
till I get paid. In this case,
I think two wrongs do make a right. Still, this key

feels wrong somehow. *Calm down. Put the key
in the lock; turn it to the right.*
I don't call this stealing, but I have a bad case
of nerves all the same. I'm only taking my own clothes
plus some cereal and cans of food
that my parents should've given me. If Dad came home from work

and caught me here, would he say, *Look, I'm sorry, let's work
this out,* or would he take my car keys
too, so I wouldn't have a place to keep the food
I "steal" from him? I don't know. Right
now, I think I better grab my clothes
and get out fast. King wants me to play. Sorry, boy, it's not a case

of me not having time for you. It's a case
where I'd like to take you with me, but it just wouldn't work.
It's hard enough to sleep and change clothes
in my car; I couldn't keep a dog. The key
to making it from one day to the next right
now is: Keep it simple. Food.

A sleeping bag. A place to park at night. The food
has to be easy to eat. I keep it covered, in case
anyone looks in my car. If I do everything just right
I can make this work.
(I hope I get a job.) Okay, where did I put the key?
I'm out of here. Clothes,

food, sleeping bag. Pillow, shampoo, towel. Close
and lock the door. Key right back where I found it.
Case closed. Go somewhere warm and do my homework.

the deep end KATIE

It snowed last night, eight inches deep.
Keesha knocked and said, *No school today*,
so I wrapped my blankets close around me
and I slept and slept. Every time
I tried to make myself wake up, something pulled
me back into the deepest sleep I've had for months.

It was noon when I woke up. I read last month's
Teen People, drank some coffee, took a long, deep
breath, and looked out at the snow. A memory pulled
me back ten years: it was snowing like today,
but colder and no wind. When's the last time
I felt that safe? Dad bundled me

up in my purple snowsuit and took me
sledding on the hill behind our house. It had been months
since he'd taken any time
off work, but that day the snow was too deep
for anyone to drive, deeper than today.
He sat behind me on our yellow sled and pulled

me close to his warm chest. We flew together down that hill, pulled
the sled back to the top. Over and over. To me,
that memory is like a clear glass marble I can hold today.
It was that same year, maybe that same month,
that, as Mom puts it, Dad *went off the deep
end*. I didn't know what she meant the first time

I heard that. All I could picture was the time
I jumped in a swimming pool and the lifeguard had to pull
me out. Mom said, *No, Katie, this is the deep
end!* But all that made no sense to me—
Dad was a good swimmer. Why was he gone for months?
Why didn't someone pull *him* out? Days like today

when I have time to remember, I understand. Today
I know what the deep end is, and there are times
I'm scared I could go off it too. Last month
when Mom's husband came in my room and pulled
me toward him, tried to put his hands all over me,
I fought back hard. I made four deep

scratches on his shoulder. I guess I went off the deep end that time,
and as of today, no one's pulled
me out. Sometimes I just want to sleep for months.

PART V

WE PASS EACH OTHER

we pass each other   STEPHIE

I first met Keesha in seventh grade
at a citywide field day where we
competed in long jump and hurdles.
I thought she could fly! I watched
her take the hurdles, one at a time,
like her life depended on clearing each one without touching.

Or was it that she refused to let anything touch
her? She won everything in eighth grade
too, and then in ninth I found out she went to Marshall. When the time
came to try out for the track team, we
both made it. She is so determined! I watch
her practice harder than everyone else and take first in hurdles

at every meet. Lately, I've been thinking about the hurdles
people face in their lives. It's like us kids are just touching
the starting line, with everybody watching
where we stand in sports and in our grades.
They measure us against each other, but no one knows what we
go through to get where we start from. The time

I spent last month at Keesha's house, and the time
talking to Mom since then, make me think about those hurdles—
those private things that no one knows about. We
judge people by certain standards that don't touch
who they really are. I know I'll get bad grades
this term, but what do they say about *me*? Is anyone watching

what I'm going through inside? Or are they only watching
how my body changes, talking about me all the time
as if they knew me: *Terrible, a girl in tenth grade*
having a baby she can't support. I wonder what hurdles
they've faced. Most of the time, we pass each other without touching.
I look at people in the halls, kids we

think are losers, and I think: We
don't know them. Everyone is watching
Jason now to see what he'll decide about next year. I can't touch
whatever is going on with him, no matter how much time
we spend talking. Is he the one I want to face life's hurdles
with? I don't even know. He gets good grades.

He's good at sports. Good-looking. Most of the time, that's all we
watch. But how does someone face an unexpected hurdle?
That touches on what counts. And there's no grade for that.

making sure   JASON

When Stephie's number showed up on my pager last night
in the locker room, I was confused.
It was the first game of the tournament, I was sure
she'd be there early, and the game was starting
in less than half an hour. I'd suited up already,
but I got to a phone and called. Her brother answered.

Dad took her to the hospital. He couldn't answer
any of my questions. That was the beginning of the longest night
of my life. Three reporters had already
interviewed me about the *big game.* I bet they were confused
when our team came out and I wasn't in the starting
lineup. Coach was furious, but I was sure

I had to be with Stephie—I surprised myself, how sure
I was. I got there in record time—*What's wrong?* She didn't answer.
She was crying. Finally she told me, *I'm starting
to bleed. I might lose the baby.* I stayed all night,
holding her hand, not talking much. I'm still a little confused
by what I learned about myself: I already

think of myself as a father. The doctor had already
examined Stephie. He came back in. *Are you sure
you want this child?* She was confused
by that. She couldn't say. I answered
to myself, *Yes, I do. I want this child.* All night
the bleeding kept stopping and then starting

again. At 4:20, just when we were starting
to think she was okay, the doctor came back in. I wasn't ready
to hear what he said: *The fetus is no longer living.* The rest of the night
everyone was in and out, just making sure
Stephie was all right. She looked at me and said, *I have my answer,*
and then she fell asleep. I was confused

by that. What answer? Today she told me, *I've been confused*
about my feelings for you. I was starting
to wonder if you're right for me. The answer
she meant was *Yes, you are.* She's home already
and neither of us is sure
how we feel about what happened last night.

Starting last November, things have gone too fast. Tonight
we're both confused by this relief and love and sadness, sure
of some answers, already facing other questions.

BURNiNG KEESHA

I don't know what to do.
Tobias came over here last night with a burn
on his arm, under his sleeve where it won't show.
I thought it was something Dad
did, and I was about to say, *Stay*
here awhile till things cool off at home.

But, turns out, it didn't happen at home,
at least not like I thought. He says all he was trying to do
was make a little money, and he meant to stay
away from drugs and gangs. But this burn
says to me, That won't be so easy for Tobias. Dad's
no help. I wish there was someone to show

my brother there's better ways to earn a living. I could show
him my little paycheck, but I can't make a home
for him. People like Jermaine and Dan step in where Dad
should be. *Look, all you gotta do . . .*
Sounds so easy. You don't see them getting burned
when these big guys get greedy. I told Tobias he could stay

here for a couple days, but he said they'd find out where he stays,
and before too long they'd show
up here. Tobias says they told him, *Next time, we burn*
your pretty li'l face. They think he's hiding drugs at home,
and he says it's not true. I've heard about these guys. They'd do
what they say, and they'd make sure to come around when Dad's

not there. Should I try to talk to Dad?
Tobias says he's drinking worse than ever. *Just stay*
outta this, Keesha. You don't hafta do
nothin' for me. I'll be okay. When he tries to show
that brave face, I see how scared he really is. This home
I have is nice enough, but it's not really mine. I bandaged up the burn,

and Tobias left, looking small and lonely. Now I'm burning
up inside about his so-called friends, our so-called dad,
and how my brother doesn't have the kind of home
he needs. Say I let him come and stay
here. Say those guys—or the cops—show
up. Then what would me and Katie do?

Not to mention Joe. I'd feel like I burned down the home
he's giving us. Joe's no dad, but he stays steady.
God, I miss Mama. She'd show us what to do.

RUNNIN' OUTTA COUCHES   DONTAY

I'm runnin' outta couches. Been
to six places in four weeks. Now
I'm startin' over at Jermaine and Dan's.
Only trouble is, Dan think I owe
him somethin' if I stay here,
so I been thinkin' hard.

I'm hungry and it's hard
to say no to the money he talkin' 'bout. They been
feedin' me whenever I come over here.
Only—I know what I decide now
I gotta live with. I could end up owin'
somethin' I ain't got, or one of Dan's

friends could tell a lie about me. Dan
won't stop 'em if they come down on me hard
like I seen 'em do Tobias, sayin' he owe
'em $300 'cause they don't like what he delivered. Tobias ain't been
'round here much since then. Now
Dan need someone new, and here

I am. *Look, all you gotta do is take this bag from here
to Seventh Street and bring me back the money.* Dan
make it sound easy, and it look that way now,
but somethin' bound to go wrong. It's harder
to get outta this than in. I been
thinkin' 'bout Dad and Mama, wonderin' what I owe

them. One time Dad told me, *All you owe
anyone is, do the best you know how.* If he was here,
what would he say? Him and Mama been
locked up two years now. If I start helpin' Dan,
I could end up inside before they get out. Hard
to say what I should do. I need money now,

but somethin' tells me, run. Right now,
I'm hungry, but I don't owe
nobody nothin'. Tobias told me it gets harder
once you start that stuff. He gave me an address: *Here's
a place my sister Keesha stays. Let Dan
get some other underage to do what I been*

doin'. He's right. I don't feel right no more here at Dan
and Jermaine's. It's hard to go somewhere I never been,
but I'm goin'. I owe Tobias a big favor now.

sometimes i wonder   CARMEN

Sometimes it seems like it don't matter
if you lie or tell the truth.
People pick out what they want to believe—
all you can do is hope they pick
the things that count. Tomorrow, I finally got my court
date. So much dependin' on which judge

I get and what he's feelin' like when I come in. One judge
knows Grandmama, and that ain't s'posed to matter,
but I can tell you, I'll be glad if he has court
tomorrow. Grandmama's been comin' to see me. She says, *Truth
is easy. You don't got so much to remember.* She picked
out a nice dress for me to wear: *Believe*

me, Carmen, it's important how you look. I do believe
that, but there's a lot about my looks that I can't change. Judge
me by my character, like Dr. King said. Well, I can't pick
my judge, and I can't change the facts, or for that matter
what they think is facts. Truth
is, I'm part guilty, part innocent, and the court

decides how to put that together. Last time I had court
I said I wasn't drinkin'—only with some kids that was. They
     believed
me, and I just got probation. Now this time, truth
is I did have one beer. I can hear that judge
already, all stern, sayin', *Young lady, this matter
before us is serious.* I know I gotta start pickin'

better friends. Anytime someone say, *We'll pick
you up for a party*, I just go along. It shouldn't take the court
to make me use more sense. What's the matter
with me, anyhow, that I don't make my own mind up? I believe
most of the things the judge
says, but sometimes I wonder, what *is* the whole truth?

I know I'm the only one that can tell myself the truth
and make me listen. If I go home, will I just pick
up where I left off, or can I change? That's for the judge
to decide, I guess. I'm hopin' I can go home after court
tomorrow and stay out of trouble. Grandmama believes
me, that I want to try. She says, *Girl, no matter*

what you do, I keep on believin' in you. She should be a judge
herself, the way she picks through lies and truth
and court talk, and comes up with that one thing that matters.

Do Not Leave Children Unattended

HARRIS

After school and on weekends I go to the library
and do my homework or listen
to music. I brush my teeth, wash my hair,
and, a couple times a week, I shave. They have
a private sink in one of the handicap stalls.
Sometimes I go in the youth section and sign

up to play computer games. There's a sign
in there: DO NOT LEAVE CHILDREN UNATTENDED IN THE LIBRARY.
I know there's younger kids than me who use the sink in that stall
like I do. I keep my eye on them. I try to listen
to adults that talk to them, especially in the rest room. Last week, I had
something creepy happen when I was combing my hair.

A guy made a comment about my *gorgeous red hair*,
which is nothing new. But right after that—the first sign
of something weird—he asked if he could have
a picture of me. I got out of there fast. When the library
was about to close, he left the same time I did. *Hey, listen,*
he said, *you need a ride somewhere?* I said, *No, thanks*, stalled

for time until he left. The next day, I came out of the stall
and he was in the rest room combing his hair.
He said something to me, but I didn't stay to listen.
Now I watch every move he makes. If I ever see a sign
that he's messing with one of the kids that hang out in the library,
I'll—well, I don't know what I'll do, but I know I'd have

to help. I guess I'd act casual, like I had
some reason to be there—but I'd stall
around and eavesdrop till he left the kid alone. The library
should be a safe place, and if a kid needs a place to comb his hair,
just let him be. Hey! I finally got a job. I'm going in to sign
the paperwork this afternoon. I have to listen

to a tape about dishwashing safety. That's funny! I've listened
to my mother harp on that stuff all my life. Like—you have
to scrub the cutting board. Use bleach or boiling water. There's a sign
in the rest room—in fact, there's one in every stall—
reminding us employees to wash our hands. We have to use hair
nets if we get anywhere near food. The librarians

won't be seeing so much of me now. That's a good sign. I'll have
a bathroom I can use at work, and I'll just use the library stall
to wash my hair. I'll listen to music while it dries.

we can both see   KATIE

1.
Once in a while, something good happens, and things fall
into place. I was getting to the point
where I thought I'd have to quit
school. I couldn't afford a car,
and I didn't have the time for that long bus ride.
Then this new guy, Harris, shows up at work.

I know him a little from school. Freshman year, we worked
together on a lab report, and once last fall
I sat with him on the bus ride
coming home from a field trip to Oak Point.
Now, it turns out, he has a car,
and I can get from school to work with him. I don't have to quit

school or my job. It's like someone's saying, *Katie, don't quit
now; you've come this far and you've worked
hard to get here.* Every afternoon, I lean back in that car
and close my eyes. Sometimes I actually fall
asleep. Of course, I make it a point
to pay for gas. I've never expected a free ride.

2. (two weeks later)
Whenever we get off work together, Harris gives me a ride
home. But I can't find out where he lives. He won't say, so I quit
asking. Maybe that's a sore point
with him, like it sort of is with me. Sometimes after work
I invite him in, and Keesha jokes around that I'm falling
in love. It isn't that, but I keep thinking about his car,

full of clothes and blankets. I bet anything he lives in that car.
I bet when it gets cold he rides
around until the car warms up, and then he falls
asleep till he gets cold again. Keesha says I should quit
worrying about other people. *You have to work
hard enough to take care of yourself!* Good point,

but I could make the same point
back to her. She says if it turns out his car
is all he's got, and if he has enough hours at work
to pay for food, next time he gives me a ride
I could let him know that if he ever wants to quit
all that, there's room here. I remember last fall,

I met Keesha at a low point in my life. I almost quit
both school and work. Through all that's happened, she never let me fall.
Now we can both see: Harris has a car, but he needs a ride.

PART VI

KEESHA'S HOUSE

keesha's house   JOE

It used to be when kids showed up they'd say,
I'm lookin' for Joe's house. Somebody sent me here
and said to ask you for a place to stay
tonight. They'd stay a week, a month, a year . . .
It's still like that, 'cept now they look at me
like, *Where'd you come from? Ain't this Keesha's house?*
I go get Keesha, and I watch while she
checks out the situation, thinks what couch
or bed we got. Time and again, she makes
the right decision. She helps so many kids.
The way she holds her head up, my heart breaks—
ain't nobody thinkin' 'bout what Keesha needs.
I love this girl whatever way I can,
too young to be her father, too old to be her man.

same old story   CHARLES (DONTAY'S FATHER)

A month now, Dontay's missing. Letter came
today—his foster father still ain't said
just why the boy run off. Sound like the same
old story: they get paid, he don't get fed.
Ain't nobody seen my boy. I know Lucille
be sick with worry too—our youngest son
in danger, us in here just prayin' he'll
be found before he mess up bad. Just one
mistake. He'll think he won't get caught. Might
be right, a time or two. But he won't stop.
Stakes get higher; can't get out; some night
somebody got no use for him. I got
two years behind me, about one more to go.
There's too much I can't see. Too much I know.

He's got a place ANTHONY (DONTAY'S FOSTER FATHER)

Sounds like Charles and Lucille are blaming us
for Dontay being gone so long. We've
tried to keep them up to date, and trust
they'll call us if he contacts them. We leave
the front porch light on every night in case
he comes back here. Lenora keeps his bed
made up, and we agree he's got a place
with us if he comes back. We must have said
something that set Dontay off—it's hard to know.
The rules that make our own kids feel secure
don't work that way for him. He has to show
how much he doesn't need us, but I'm not so sure.
There's so many things he should be told
but he can't hear them. Fourteen years old.

WHO'Ð BE HURT? JUDGE DAVISON

The juvenile system is set up
to protect kids and the community at large.
I don't see it as either "pass a cup
of kindness" or "put the monsters behind bars."
Take Carmen: I read her case and try to judge
what she did, what she intended, what she knew.
She's not perfect. There's a little smudge
or two in here I can't ignore. But who
would I be helping by coming down too hard?
Who'd be hurt by letting her go home?
I weigh the facts, decide what I regard
as truth, and think what I'd want for my own
child. I believe Carmen will be okay.
I'll talk straight, then send her on her way.

she's doing okay WILLIAM (KEESHA'S FATHER)

Tobias knows the place where Keesha stays,
that house on Jackson Street with a blue door.
She's prob'ly better off there. Still, some days
I wonder—if I went over there and swore
I'd stay sober: first, would she come home?
and second, could I keep my word?
Sounds like she's doing okay on her own,
and why should she believe me now? Third
time I've been through this. The other two
I lasted a few weeks, then let someone talk
me into *just one drink*. Twelve Steps. That shoe
fits some people, but it's not the way I walk.
Love holds up an angry fist to pride;
they beat each other down till I'm half dead inside.

where's Harris? JEANNINE (HARRIS'S MOTHER)

Hey, King, come here. You miss him too, I know.
The house has been so quiet since he left.
You were a puppy when he was a boy, and now
we're both getting old. Where's Harris? What Greg calls the *theft*
of his blankets and clothes at least lets me hope he's warm.
I keep setting his place and cooking for three. More
for you, I suppose . . . 3:17 . . . An alarm
goes off—you hear it too—each day when the door
stays closed. Harris is not choosing this. Greg's wrong.
I've read enough books by now to know.
Could Greg change his mind? It could take a long
time. Does Harris have any safe place to go?
All these questions, and who am I talking to?
King, the only one listening seems to be you.

skating off aLone   MARTHA (KATIE'S MOTHER)

I dreamed of Katie skating in the blue
costume I wore when I was seventeen.
Someone pushed her and she fell—who
was it? She sprawled on the ice, weeping, between
two skaters who went sailing on, leaving me—
I mean *her*—leaving Katie there. Who's this Joe
who lets these kids stay in his house for free?
Could he be molesting Katie? *No,*
Mom, no one's hurting us. This place
is safe. She's clear on that. But why so cold
toward me? She gets that look on her face
like I should know what's wrong without being told.
In the dream, she slammed down the phone.
Then she—or was it me?—went skating off alone.

PART VII

FINDING HEARTBEATS

keesha's brother

Oh, God! It's Keesha's brother in the paper.
Front page story: *Tobias Walker, age*
fourteen, was found dead Tuesday afternoon
outside a house on Seventh Street.
An investigation is under way. Witnesses are asked
to come forward. Oh, Keesha . . . Her brother

was a nice kid, decent. The little brother
she was always trying to keep track of. This paper
will be in everybody's hands today—she'll be asked
the same questions over and over. My brother
is the same age as hers. He goes down that street
to go swimming at the Y every Monday afternoon.

Mr. Hyde pulled Keesha out of practice yesterday afternoon—
that must have been when she heard about her brother.
She left in tears without a word to anyone. What a lonely street
my friend walks down, with nothing but a paper-
thin umbrella keeping out the rain. This age
we are—it's supposed to be so fun, but if you ask

me, it's really hard. When I lost the baby, I asked
myself a lot of questions, and then one afternoon
it came to me: I can act my age
again! I'm a *girl* with a mom and a dad and a brother
and *no baby*, and I better get my research paper
done for English class. I felt like skipping down the street,

laughing and shouting: *Look, everyone! Our streets
are paved with gold!* Coach Johnson asked,
What's gotten into you? I got an A on my research paper
and I thought the whole world was mine. This afternoon,
my feet are on the ground again. If someone's brother
can be here one day and gone the next at age

fourteen, I feel like I don't want to be this age
too long. I just want to cross the street
before the light turns red, get home and tell my brother
to stay inside where he'll be safe. I asked
Jason to go with me to the funeral Sunday afternoon,
and he said yes, although to him it's just a story in the paper.

Tobias Walker, age fourteen, found dead. Has anyone asked
what Tobias was doing on that street on a school-day afternoon?
Keesha's brother! Most people will read this and toss out the paper.

iNVisiBLe sHieLƌ JASON

I didn't even know Tobias Walker,
but this funeral shook me up. He looked
like a child, lying in that casket, wearing
a clean white shirt, eyes closed
like he was sleeping, except he
had this defiant expression on his face, as if to say,

I don't care what you do to me. I wanted to say,
*Come back and try again. Walk
back here—give the world another chance.* He
almost seemed like he could hear what I was thinking. I looked
over at his sister, sitting in the front row, arms closed
across her chest, eyes blazing, wearing

an expression like a volcano about to erupt. She was wearing
a dark suit that made her look older than she is. I wanted to say
something to her that might come close
to being right, but what? After the funeral, I walked
out ahead of Stephie, and when I looked
back, I saw Steph reach out, heard her say to Keesha, *He . . .*

then stop and step back. That one word, *he,*
was more than Keesha could hear. It was like she was wearing
some kind of invisible shield. Stephie looked
like she was trying hard to think of what to say,
but, like me, she couldn't. Keesha walked
away and got into a car. A guy closed

the car door and drove off. *Who's that, that closed
the door?* I asked, and Stephie said, *That's Joe. He
owns the house.* Later we went for a long walk
down by the river, and she told me more about the house where
Keesha and some other kids live on their own. *Don't say
anything to any grownups*, Stephie said. *Look,*

I said, *they shouldn't have to do this! Look
at all the agencies set up to help.* It's a closed
subject to Stephie. She promised Keesha not to say
anything, especially about Joe. He knows some people think he
should report the kids, but he's not going to. It's wearing
on me, thinking about them, and then about Tobias Walker.

At least Joe doesn't close his door and walk away. He does what he
can. It looks to me like the kids at Keesha's house are wearing
lives designed for people twice their age. But what, if anything,
  should I say?

a good person KEESHA

When we were little kids, Tobias liked to hide
and make me try to find him. He was good
at hiding; he never made a sound
to give himself away. Sometimes I'd keep
looking for a *long* time before I'd see
some small movement, and then his little grin. I can still

see it. Tonight I have to make myself sit still
and not look everywhere he could be hiding,
hoping I might find him. If I could just see
him one last time, smiling that good-
natured smile—if I could say goodbye—I might not keep
thinking he's alive somewhere. I might not jump at every sound,

thinking it's my brother calling me. Now it sounds
like Joe's home. I'm surprised he's still
letting me stay here, after what I did last night. I keep
expecting—I don't even know. What happens if I don't always hide
the way I'm feeling? Joe's gotta be a good
man to stand by and see

me lose control that bad and still see
something good in me. It all started with the sound
of that red cup breaking on the kitchen floor. It felt good
to hear it break. I dropped another cup and then another, and it still
felt good. Threw three plates on the floor and didn't try to hide
the pieces. Felt like, if I could keep

on breaking dishes, maybe I could keep
myself from breaking. I wonder—who did Joe see
when he walked in? I didn't even try to hide
what I was doing, and by that time, some sound
was coming out of me. I still
don't know where it got started—it felt good

and awful all at once. Joe grabbed my wrists, held them. *You are a good*
person, Keesha. It's okay. You just keep
on cryin'. Was I crying? I held still
then and let Joe hold me. I let him see
me cry, let him hear that ugly sound.
Didn't even try to hide.

Maybe Tobias used to keep on hiding
just to hear the sound of me still looking.
Tonight I see how getting found feels good.

ready to try again DONTAY

Only three days after I got to Keesha's house,
we heard what happened to Tobias. I never
felt so scared. I don't even want
to know who did it, or when, or how,
or why. Just wanna keep my distance
from the whole mess. It could

be me, buried six feet deep, and Tobias could
be sleepin' on this couch in Keesha's house.
Seems like, sometimes, ain't no distance
between life and death, even if you never
mean to go that way. Keesha started sayin' how
I should find out if my foster parents want

me back. She'd say, *You should call, at least. I bet they want
to know where you're at.* Sure, but how could
I do it? I knew they'd be plenty mad, how
I stayed gone all this time. One thing about their house
though—I know it's safe. I started wishin' I never
left—might be good to put some distance

between me and Dan. But it's a long distance
between wishin' and doin', and even when I wanted
to go back, I could never
get myself to make that call. I could
tell myself to do it, picture the phone ringin' at their house,
but I could never picture how

they'd answer. Joe must've been watchin' how
I'd pick up the phone and put it down. Could he see the distance
I was feelin' between this house
and that one? Finally, last night, he called there himself. *I want
to speak to Dontay's foster father.* How could
he do that so easy when he never

even met him? The two of 'em talked awhile. I never
even had to apologize or nothin'. Heard Joe say, *How
can you make rules that work for you, that Dontay could
learn to live with?* Man, there's a big distance
between kids and grownups. If I wanted
to talk like that, I'd never know the words. This house

is pretty far from that house, but when I said I wanted
to go back, they said I could. Look at the distance
between *never* and how I'm ready to try again today.

a LONG, HARD taLk   CARMEN

Grandmama sat me down for a long, hard talk
the day after the judge sent me home.
She said, *We gotta get to the bottom*
of this drinkin' business. Tell me why
you started and how you plan to stop.
I went back in my mind to that first

time, when I was twelve, the first
day of summer vacation. I let this girl talk
me into goin' to a party with some older kids. *Stop*
right there, Grandmama said. *Whose party? Were the parents home?*
The whole time we talked, she was like that: *Who? Why?*
When? Strange thing is, I wasn't mad. At the bottom

of all her questions was one thing—love—and the bottom
line is, I figured out by now, that's the first
thing I need. Truth is, I don't know exactly why
I started drinkin'. Just fun, I guess. You're talkin'
to someone, they hand you a beer, and by the time you go home
you've had more than you meant to. You don't stop

to think about it at the time. *Okay, but can you stop*
when you decide to? She kept pushin', gettin' to the bottom
of everything I said. That one scared me, 'cause when I got home
even after all that thinkin' I been doin', the first
thing on my mind was: Who's around that I can talk
into buyin' me some beer? Before I answered Grandmama, I said, *Why*

you need to know that? Wasn't bein' sassy, just had to know why
this was so important. She stopped
a minute. Somethin' was hard for her to talk
about. Then she said, *Your grandpa and your auntie both hit bottom
over this.* (Didn't mention Mama.) *If it's hard for you, you ain't the first
one in our family. Nothin' wrecks a happy home*

faster than addiction. That's somethin' I want—a happy home—
and that word—*addiction*—might be why
this whole thing's been so hard. Once I take that first
drink, it's like Grandmama thought, I can't stop
until the party's over and I see the bottom
of the bottle. I need some help on this, someone to talk

me into takin' that first step. Talkin'
about *why* is one thing; stayin' home from parties is another.
I want to stop now, not wait till I hit bottom.

Light through the window   HARRIS

By the time Katie figured out I was living
in my car, I'd saved some money. Enough
so when they asked me if I wanted to move in, I could buy
a bed that folds into a couch during the day.
I found this little room with a window,
up in the attic, and Joe said I could sleep up here.

Now if I want to be alone, I can come up here
and it's not lonely, because I hear sounds of people living
downstairs in the house. Outside my window
a maple tree is starting to leaf out—it lets in just enough
light to make these dancing shadows on the wall every day
when I wake up. I didn't have to buy

too much. I've learned what I can live without. I might buy
a small rug or something, but first I'll look around up here.
Joe's aunt Annie left lots of trunks and boxes full of stuff. One day
I dusted off an old chess set and brought it down to the living
room. Katie knows how to play, and Joe plays well enough
to give us both a challenge. Yesterday Keesha stood by the window

watching a game between Katie and me. Light through the window
made her face look softer than it used to. By
the time she'd watched a couple games, she knew enough
to try a game herself. It's like having sisters, being here.
I called Mom where she works and told her I'm living
with some friends and doing okay. The next day

we met downtown for lunch. She said ever since the day
Dad threw me out, she's been trying to find some window
she can open in his mind. When someone's lived
as long as he has, thinking one way, it's hard to buy
into something new. I listened to her. But now I'm sitting here
thinking, *Blah, blah, blah.* Neither of my parents has enough

backbone to stand up for me when they see I'm not enough
like the kid they wish I was. Maybe some day
I'll feel more forgiving, but right now, right here,
as far as I'm concerned, Mom can take her little window
to Dad's mind and slam it shut in both their faces. She wants to buy
me stuff. *Do you need new clothes? Is the place you're living*

safe? You know what? I have enough of everything. The day
I moved in here, I took a shower and went out to buy
a bed. I'm living in a house with open windows.

fin∂iɴɢ ʜeaʀtʙeats   KATIE

Since Harris got here, we've all been finding
things up in the attic and having fun
putting them around the house. A polished turtle shell
wrapped in comics from 1962. Lennon Sisters
paper dolls, must be from the fifties; old
vinyl Elvis records and a record player we can play

them on. Keesha brought down a box of shoes and hats and we played
dress-up just like little kids. I keep going up and finding
things to bring down to my room. A bed frame and an old
blue quilt, a purple lamp shade, and this funny
yellow frog that croaks when I open my door. Joe says his sister
took all the useful stuff. He said the house was just a shell

with a few pieces of ugly furniture after she went through it. She'll
come over sometimes and talk to Joe: *Remember how they used to play
the piano and sing, Aunt Annie and her sisters?*
Joe remembers coming home from school and finding
them all laughing and talking and having fun
around this same beat-up old

table in the kitchen. But I found some old
diaries Aunt Annie kept, and under that shell
of singing and laughing, everything wasn't all fun.
One time she tried out for a school play—
she wrote about working really hard, and then finding
out that all the time she thought her sister

was helping her, she was planning to try out too. Her sister
got the part that Annie wanted, and Annie got the part of an old
lady, ugly and mean. Annie wrote that finding
out what Rosa did made her furious, but she made a hard shell
around those feelings and found a way to use them in the play.
Around Rosa, she acted like it was all in fun

even though they both knew it wasn't. Rosa thought it was fun
to see who she could hurt. All my life I've wanted a sister,
but who's to say you'd get one you could trust? Playing
dress-up with Keesha is like finding a sister when I'm old
enough to pick a good one. We took that turtle shell
and put it on a table, and everyone's been finding

ways to use it—some funny, some serious. Last night Harris played
it with his palms and fingertips, like it was an old drum. That shell
was finding heartbeats in this house: sister/sister/brother/friend.

PART VIII

PAINT AND PAINTBRUSH

the wide blue door   STEPHIE

Keesha's house is set back off the street
so if you don't know what you're looking for
you might not even see the wide blue door
half hidden by a weeping willow tree.
Tonight I knocked and Harris answered. He
wasn't here when I was here before,
that one weekend last winter. It's been more
than six months since then, and I was three
months pregnant at the time. I do this math
a lot: When would the baby have been born?
Who would she be? I'm half—no, more than half—
glad how it turned out. But something's torn
somewhere inside me. These friends help me laugh
when I need laughter. This kitchen's warm.

is it fair? JASON

When I need laughter, their kitchen's warm,
Steph says. I went to Keesha's house with her
but it didn't make me laugh. Sure,
they're okay now, but things go wrong—some storm
coming, a couple miles offshore, torn-
up roof—torn lives. But I won't refer
them to authorities, don't want to stir
up trouble. We all want freedom. The form
it takes for me is leaving home to go
to college, paying my way with basketball,
all my expenses, all four years. I know
my dad will drive me out there in the fall
and back at Christmas. I'm grateful, and I show
it. Sometimes I wonder if it's fair, that's all.

shifting gears KEESHA

Sometimes I wonder if it's fair, all
the stuff that's happened in my life so far.
How do people find out who they are,
who they're meant to be? I want to call
time-out, hit pause or rewind, stop the ball—
no, stop the bullet—in midair.
I want Tobias back, safe in a car
with someone sober driving, someone tall
enough to see beyond the next few years,
see us both alive, safe, grown,
and say: *Tobias. Keesha. It's okay.*
But—looks like I'm the driver. I shift gears,
head uphill with all the life I've got—my own.
I might do something about all this someday.

tHRee montHs DONTAY

I might do somethin' about all this someday—
how in my foster home I'm like a pet
they know they can get rid of if I get
ornery. But for now I'm doin' okay.
We talked, I made up my mind to stay,
and if they pull that stuff, I try to let
it roll off my back. Do you s'pose ducks get wet
when water rolls off them? Who knows? Hey—
know what? I'm almost happy. Heard from Dad—
they're prob'ly gettin' out in three months' time.
Time off for good behavior. I know he's had
to put up with worse'n I have. I'm
behavin' myself too. It ain't so bad.
Three months. That's a mountain I can climb.

one step higher CARMEN

Three months now on this mountain. I can climb
it step by step. I say no to a drink;
I'm one step higher. I stop and think
before I head out to a party. Fine
with me if they stop askin'. Old friends of mine
say I ain't fun no more. Used to sink
into a funk about that. Now I hardly blink.
Dontay still comes by a lot. He's tryin'
to stay clear of trouble too. He knows some kids
at Keesha's house on Jackson Street, and none
of 'em is into drinkin'. Friday nights he heads
down there, and lately I go too. I made one
good decision three months back. It spreads
its light ahead of me, and I walk on.

up to us   HARRIS

There's light ahead of me as I walk on
into my senior year. I wasn't sure
about going back, but Katie said, *If you're
about to quit, The Jerks will think they won.*
She calls them that—The Jerks—like Dontay calls me son
when he gives me fake advice: *Stay pure,
son, in thought word and deed. We'll find a cure
for you someday.* I laugh. It's all in fun.
If people we're supposed to count on can't
(or don't) support us, it's up to us to find
the friends who can and do. Of course we want
to be with both our parents in the kind
of home where we'd be loved. But why rant
on about all that? Home is in your mind.

paint and paintbrush   KATIE

About all that *Home is in your mind*
stuff Harris talks about: It's true—
like how I kept picturing a blue-
and-yellow room before I painted mine
like this to match what I imagined.
Still, I had to have the paint and paintbrush too.
Keesha's talking about what she'll do
for kids someday. Take that dream and wind
it up with some of what she needs: she will
do something big. Or maybe something sweet
and small that no one knows about. I'll
be listening someday when two kids meet:
Look for flowers on the windowsill—
Keesha's House is set back off the street.

NOTES ON THE FORMS
ACKNOWLEDGMENTS

NOTES ON THE FORMS

All of the poems in *Keesha's House* have been written in traditional poetic forms. These forms have been handed down for generations, and each brings its own gifts and power to the writer and, in turn, to the reader. The forms are something like houses that allow exploration within their kitchens, living rooms, attics, and basements. Often, the rules of a form provide a distraction from what a writer intends to say, leading to more interesting images and ideas.

Here are the traditional rules of each form. If you look carefully at my poems, you will find places where I have been playful with these rules and places where I have bent them or occasionally ignored them for the sake of allowing the poem to speak its mind. Always, the character who speaks the poem has the final say.

sestina

The sestina is a French form in which six words are repeated in a particular order as the end words of each line in six 6-line stanzas. Then the same six words are used one more time in a 3-line stanza, or envoi, which concludes the poem. Traditionally, all the lines have the same number of syllables, but I have chosen to vary the length of the lines in these poems. I have followed the traditional order of the words through the six stanzas, but in the final envoi, I have used the words in any order.

The order of the end words (each letter stands for a word) is *abcdef, faebdc, cfdabe, ecbfad, deacfb, bdfeca.* The traditional order of the end words in the three lines of the envoi is *be, dc, fa.* (The first of the two words is somewhere within the line, and the second word ends the line.)

sonnet

The sonnet is a fourteen-line poem. Each line has a given meter, or rhythm, known as iambic pentameter (daDA, daDA, daDA, daDA, daDA), and a set rhyme pattern. In the following rhyme patterns, each letter stands for a rhyme sound. In the sonnets in this book, I have used some half rhymes and near rhymes.

An English sonnet (also called an Elizabethan, or Shakespearean, sonnet) rhymes *abab cdcd efef gg.* The poems in Part VI are English sonnets.

The Italian sonnet (also called a Petrarchan sonnet) rhymes *abbaabba cdcdcd* or *abbaabba cdecde.*

A crown of sonnets is a set of seven Italian sonnets, linked through repeated lines. The last line of one sonnet is the first line of the next (sometimes with minor variations), and the last line of the last sonnet circles back to the first line of the first sonnet. Part VIII is a crown of sonnets.

A hybrid sonnet is half English and half Italian. The poems in Part III are hybrid sonnets, with most of them rhyming *abba cddc efgefg.* There are other ways of combining the different elements of a sonnet to create hybrid sonnets.

ACKNOWLEDGMENTS

I have received a great deal of support while I have worked on these poems; this book would not have been completed without it.

The time I needed for writing the book was supported by the Mary Anderson Center for the Arts, the Anderson Center at Tower View, the Indiana Arts Commission, and the National Endowment for the Arts. Through the IAC fellowship I received, I was able to pay several youth consultants who gave me valuable insights into the characters' situations and language. Thank you, Alyson Beery, Teia Hackley, Joel Miller, Damionne Nichols, and Joi Perry.

I am also grateful for the adult readers, friends, and consultants who encouraged me with their enthusiasm, questions, suggestions, information, and understanding. Ketu Oladuwa read the manuscript section by section as I was writing, and his perceptions about the characters were invaluable. Others who have been especially helpful are Julia Brita, Dave Brittenham, Ann Colbert, Susan Dailey, Claire Ewart, Denise Jordan, Naida Kirkpatrick, Don Mager, Barbara Morrow, John and Beth Murphy-Beams, Mary Quigley, Doreen Rappaport, April Pulley Sayre, Lola Schaefer, Margaret Schrepfer, Judge Steven Sims, Lisa Tsetse, Ken Watson, Leigh Westerfield, Ingrid Wendt, and many staff members in places where I have met young people. I thank the Allen County Public Library and the Holiday Inn in Goshen, Indiana, for offering space for writers to meet.

I am enormously grateful to Frances Foster, Janine O'Malley, and others at Farrar Straus Giroux for thoughtful, insightful, delicate editing and for all they do to move these words between writer and reader.

I am grateful to my parents and my siblings, for the heartbeats of my childhood home. I thank my husband, Chad Thompson, and our sons, Lloyd and Glen, for their support throughout the writing of this book.

And I am grateful to the student in Haines, Alaska, who asked, upon hearing a few of the poems, "How do you know these kids?" His question suggests that the characters seemed as real to him as they do to me. Although the characters are fictional, everything that happens to them has happened to someone, somewhere. I have listened to thousands of young people share the stories of their lives in conversation and in writing, and I am grateful to them for the courage they show in situations such as the ones I have written about. I hope that they will one day write their own stories, but for now, these poems are my tribute to them.

A CONVERSATION WITH HELEN FROST

When did you realize you wanted to be a writer?
I've always loved the creatures of the world and the words that describe them. My love of writing began as soon as I could hold a stubby crayon, and it grew with me as I entered my adult life—I don't recall any one moment of realization that writing would be my primary life work.

And in particular, what drew you to poetry?
Poetry moves through things of the world, into ideas, emotions, and deep connections. It drew me to itself.

What sparked your imagination for _Keesha's House_?
Although the characters in _Keesha's House_ are fictional, I spent many hours, in many places, listening with deep respect to teens who were struggling with hard problems. This led me to imagine a place where they might find help and support. Then the characters moved in and came to have lives of their own as the story took shape in my mind.

What do you want readers to remember about your books?
Something beautiful and true that they find in the language.

Is there anything specific you would like readers to pull from this book?
I hope my readers will know that they are seen and appreciated, whoever they are, whatever their own life experience.

Which of the characters in _Keesha's House_ is most like you?
There's something of myself in each character:

Like Harris, I sometimes feel that I live in the world differently than most people.

Like Katie, if someone is hurting me, I walk away from them.

Like Stephie, I'm determined to make my own decisions, even when people who love me question those decisions. (This was more true when I was a teenager than it is now.)

Like Carmen, I've made some big mistakes and learned from them.

Like Jason, I sometimes have to make decisions that require me to balance my career with my responsibility to those I love.

Like Dontay, I'm at my best in an atmosphere of genuine acceptance.

Like Keesha, I've learned that sometimes it's not possible to prevent something bad from happening to someone I love. And also like Keesha, it's easier for me to help others than to ask for help when I need it.

It seems to me that most readers respond to the book in this way—finding something of themselves in each of the characters. When the characters' voices are linked in the final crown of sonnets, readers may feel these different aspects of themselves coming together in friendship, as the characters do.

A NEW POEM FOR READERS OF
KEESHA'S HOUSE

a sLow step

If some night you walk down a street
so deep inside a chorus of sad voices
that you cannot—simply can't—look up,
and it all seems impossible,
too late, unforgivable and no way out;
if you've already walked right past
whatever light there is: see if you can
let one foot come to rest on a smooth stone—
can you feel the ancient warmth
pressed into it? Take another step,
a slow step, another,
      another,
           and another.

This poem was published, with an accompanying photograph, in an e-book anthology that can be found by putting these words into a search engine: "Poetry Tag Time for Teens, Sylvia Vardell and Janet Wong, Editors."

TRY WRITING A TRITINA

Have you tried writing a sestina? I know you can do it, and I think you'll enjoy trying.

But if you think the sestina is too much of a challenge, here's a form you could try first.

A "tritina" is something like a sestina, but with three endwords instead of six.

TRITINA FORM

*Ten-line poem
*Three three-line stanzas and one one-line stanza.
*The endwords (last words in the lines) repeat in this pattern:

_____Word A
_____Word B
_____Word C

_____Word C
_____Word A
_____Word B

_____Word B
_____Word C
_____Word A

_____Words A, B, and C
(Use all three words in the last line.)

Note: An example of a tritina, along with examples of twenty-three other poetic forms, and descriptions of the forms, can be found in my book *Spinning Through the Universe*, also published by Frances Foster Books/Farrar Straus Giroux. Work sheets of some of the forms can be found on my Web site: helenfrost.net.

Twelve-year-old Willow stumbles upon disaster when
she mushes a dog team to her grandparents' house.
Can an unusual set of friends make things right again?

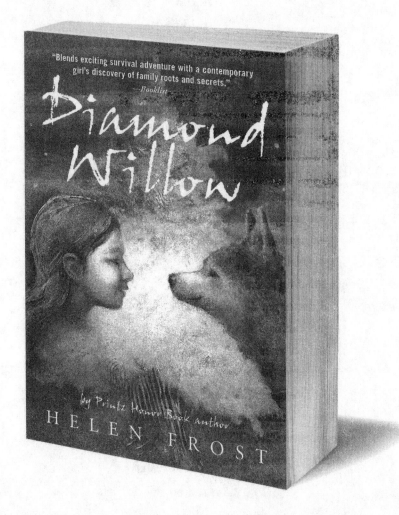

"Blends exciting survival adventure with a contemporary
girl's discovery of family roots and secrets."
—*Booklist*

*Diamond
Willow*

by *Printz Honor Book* author
HELEN FROST

Turn the page to read an excerpt from

Diamond Willow

by HELEN FROST.

In
the
middle
of my family
in the middle of
a middle-size town
in the middle of Alaska,
you will **find** middle-size,
middle-kid, **me**. My father
teaches science in the middle
of my middle school. My mother
is usually in the middle of my house.
My brother, Marty, taller and smarter
than I ever hope to be, goes to college in
big-city Fairbanks. My sister, Zanna (short
for Suzanna), is six years younger and
twelve inches shorter than I am.
She follows me everywhere—
except for the dog yard.
I don't know why
my little sister is
so scared of
dogs.

What
I love
about dogs:
They don't talk
behind your back.
If they're mad at you,
they bark a couple times
and get it over with. It's true
they slobber on you sometimes.
(I'm glad **people** don't do that.) They
jump out and **scare** you in the dark. (I know,
I should say **me**, not "you"—some people aren't
afraid of anything.) But dogs don't make fun
of you. They don't hit you in the back
of your neck with an ice-covered
snowball, and if they did, and
it made you cry, all their
friends wouldn't stand
there laughing
at you.
(Me.)

Three
votes! Did they
have to announce that?
Why not just say, *Congratulations*
to our new Student Council representative,
Richard Olenka. **Why** say how many votes each
person got (12, 7, 3)? I **don't** know why I decided to
run in the first place. A couple **people** said I should,
and I thought, Why not? (I don't **like** staying after
school, and no one would listen to **me** even if
I did have anything to say, which I don't.)
Now here I am, home right after school,
and as soon as we finish feeding
the dogs, Dad says, *Willow,*
could you help me clean
out the woodshed?
I say, *Okay,* but
it feels like
I'm getting
punished
for being
a loser.

We're
cleaning
the woodshed,
and I lift up a tarp.
An old gray stick falls out.
Just a stick. **Why** does it even catch
my eye? *Dad, what **is** this?* I turn it over in
my hands a few times; **Dad** studies it for a couple
minutes, and then he gets **so excited** he almost pops.
*Willow, let me tell you **about** this! What you have
found is more than just **an old** stick. This is the
diamond willow **stick** I found that afternoon,
just before you were born! Can it be—
let's see—twelve years ago already?
All this time, I thought it was lost.*
He hands it back to me like it's
studded with real diamonds.
*This belongs to you now.
Use your sharpest knife
to skin off the bark.
Find the diamonds.
Polish the whole
thing. It will
be beautiful,*
Dad says.
*You'll
see.*

I
came
out here to
the mudroom
so I could be alone
and make a mess while I
think my own thoughts and
skin the bark off my stick. But it's
impossible to be alone in this house.
Mom: *Willow, don't use that sharp knife*
when you're mad. I say, *I'm not mad, Mom,*
just leave me alone! and she looks at me like
I proved her point. Then, on my very next cut,
the knife slips and I rip my jeans (not too bad;
luckily, Mom doesn't seem to notice). Maybe I
should go live with **Grandma**. I bet she'd let me
stay out there with her **and Grandpa**. She could
homeschool me. I **think** I'd do better in math if
I didn't worry about how **I'm** going to get a bad
grade while Kaylie gets her **perfect** grades on
every test, then shows me her stupid paper,
and asks how I did, and, if I show her,
offers to help me figure out where
I went wrong, "so you can
do better next time,
Willow."

I

want

to mush

the dogs out

to Grandma and

Grandpa's. By myself.

I know the way. I've been

there about a hundred times

with Dad and Mom, and once

with Marty when he lived at home.

Their cabin is close to the main trail.

I know **I'm not** going to get lost, and I

won't see **a baby** moose or any bears this

time of year. Even if I did, I'd know enough

to get out of the way, fast. But Mom and

Dad don't seem to see it this way. What

do they think will happen? Dad at least

thinks about it: *She's twelve years old;*

it's twelve miles. Maybe we could

let her try. Mom doesn't

even pause for half a

second before

she says,

No

!

Maybe
they'll let me go
if I just take three dogs,
and leave three dogs here for Dad.
I'd take Roxy, of course—she's smart
and fast and she thinks the same way I do.
Magoo is fun. He doesn't have much experience,
but if I take Cora, she'd help Magoo settle down.
Dad would want one fast dog. **I'll** leave Samson
here with him. Lucky might **try** to get loose
and follow me down the trail **again**, like
the last time we left her, but this time
Dad will be here to help Mom
get her back. Prince can be
hard to handle; it will be
easier without him.
If Dad sees how
carefully I'm
thinking this
through, he
might help
convince
Mom.

I
beg
Mom:
Please!
I'd only take
three dogs. You know
I can handle them. You've
seen me. She won't listen. *You*
are not old enough, she says. *Or*
strong enough. I make a face (should
not have done that). Mom starts in: *A moose*
will charge at three dogs as fast as it will charge
at six. A three-dog team can lose the trail, or pull you
out onto thin ice. What if your sled turns over, or you lose
control of the team? (**Mom** really goes on and on once she gets
started.) *Willow, you **could be** alone out there with a dog fight*
on your hands. (Oh, **right**, Mom, like I've never stopped a
dog fight by myself.) When Mom finally stops talking
and starts thinking, I know enough to quit arguing.
She looks me up and down like we've just met,
then takes a deep breath. *You really want to*
do this, don't you, Willow? It takes me by
surprise, and I almost say, *Never mind,*
Mom, it doesn't matter. But it does
matter. I swallow hard and nod.
Mom says, *I'll think about it*
and decide tomorrow.
What if she says
yes?

You

would

trust her

to take Roxy

by herself? Mom

questions Dad. They

don't know I'm listening.

I know my dogs, Dad answers,

*how **they** are with Willow. It's more*

*that I'd **trust** Roxy to take her. Honey, if*

*it's up to **me**, I say let's let her do this.*

I slip away before they see me.

I'm pretty sure they're

going to say yes.

(Yes!)

I go out

and talk to Roxy

and Cora and Magoo.

I think they're going to let us go

to Grandma and Grandpa's by ourselves!

I get out at noon on Friday—it's the end of the

quarter. We'll leave by one, and be there before dark.

We'll have almost two days out there, and come home

Sunday afternoon! Even as **I** let myself say it,

I'm trying not to **hope** too hard.

I know all **I can do** now is

wait. **It** will jinx

it for sure if

I keep on

begging.

Yes,
I have a
wool sweater
under my jacket.
Extra socks, gloves,
and, yes, I have enough
booties for the dogs. I have
my sleeping bag and a blanket,
in case I get stranded somewhere
(which of course won't happen). *Yes,*
I have matches, a headlamp, a hatchet.
Dad keeps adding things to his checklist.
Zanna comes up as close as she dares, keeping
her distance from the dogs, to give me a card she
made for Grandma. It's cute, a picture of an otter
sliding down a riverbank. ***Okay***, Dad says, *it looks*
*like you're all set. I know you **can** do this. Take it*
slow. He keeps on talking as **I** take my foot off
the brake and let the dogs **go**. He might still
be talking even **now**, yelling out last-
minute warnings: *Don't forget to*
call us when you get there!
Watch where the trail . . .
And I can picture Mom,
standing beside Dad,
her arms folded tight,
like she's holding
me, wrapped
up inside
them.

Fox
tracks,
new snow,
red-streaked sky
and full moon rising.
I know **this** trail, know
where it **gets scary**. I know
where it **sometimes** floods and
freezes over. **And I** know Grandma
and Grandpa will **love it** when they hear
the dogs, knowing that it's me mushing
out to see them. I'm almost there.
Can't be more than half an hour
to go. Down this small
hill, past the burned
stumps. There—I
see the light
by their
door.

ALSO AVAILABLE
FROM SQUARE FISH BOOKS

Even with the odds against them, these girls never give up hope.

In the Name of God
Paula Jolin
ISBN 978-0-312-38455-5

How far would you go to
defend your beliefs?

Make Lemonade
Virginia Euwer Wolff
ISBN 978-0-8050-8070-4

Fourteen-year-old LaVaughn is
determined to go to college—she
just needs the money to get there.

A Room on Lorelei Street
Mary E. Pearson
ISBN 978-0-312-38019-9

Can seventeen-year-old Zoe
make it on her own?

Side Effects
Amy Goldman Koss
ISBN 978-0-312-60276-5

Isabelle is living a normal life
until everything changes in an
instant when she is diagnosed
with lymphoma.

Standing Against the Wind
Traci L. Jones
ISBN 978-0-312-62293-0

Patrice dreams of a first-class
education, but right now she's just
got to survive the walk to school.

Under the Persimmon Tree
Suzanne Fisher Staples
ISBN 978-0-312-37776-2

Two people trying to
find their way home find
each other along the way.

SQUARE FISH
MACTEENBOOKS.COM
AVAILABLE WHEREVER BOOKS ARE SOLD

Discover These Powerful Printz Award–Winning Books Available from Square Fish

HOLE IN MY LIFE
978-0-312-64157-3

"A memoir, by turns harrowing and hilarious, about a huge mistake."
—*The Miami Herald*

SPEAK
978-0-312-67439-7

★"*Speak* will hold readers from first word to last." —*Horn Book*, starred review

KEESHA'S HOUSE
978-0-312-64127-6

"Spare, eloquent, and elegantly concise."
—*VOYA*

REVOLVER
978-0-312-54797-4

"A gripping thriller."
—*The Guardian* (UK)

AMERICAN BORN CHINESE
978-0-312-38448-7

"Gene Luen Yang has created that rare article: a youthful tale with something new to say about American youth."
—*The New York Times Book Review*

CHARLES AND EMMA
978-0-312-66104-5

"This is the 'wow' biography on the Darwins—meticulously researched, richly rendered and rewarding every step of the way."
—*San Francisco Chronic*